HANS CHRISTIAN ANDERSEN'S

# The Little Mermaid

ADAPTED AND ILLUSTRATED BY

## RACHEL ISADORA

PUFFIN BOOKS

*For Gillian,*

*with special, special thanks to Kathy Dawson*

PUFFIN BOOKS
Published by the Penguin Group
Penguin Putnam Books for Young Readers, 345 Hudson Street, New York, New York 10014, U.S.A.
Penguin Books Ltd, 27 Wrights Lane, London W8 5TZ, England
Penguin Books Australia Ltd, Ringwood, Victoria, Australia
Penguin Books Canada Ltd, 10 Alcorn Avenue, Toronto, Ontario, Canada M4V 3B2
Penguin Books (N.Z.) Ltd, 182-190 Wairau Road, Auckland 10, New Zealand

Penguin Books Ltd, Registered Offices: Harmondsworth, Middlesex, England

First published in the United States of America by G. P. Putnam's Sons, a division of The Putnam & Grosset Group, 1998
Published by Puffin Books, a division of Penguin Putnam Books for Young Readers, 2000

1 3 5 7 9 10 8 6 4 2

THE LIBRARY OF CONGRESS HAS CATALOGED THE G. P. PUTNAM'S SONS EDITION AS FOLLOWS:
Isadora, Rachel. The little mermaid / Hans Christian Andersen; retold by Rachel Isadora.   p.   cm.
Summary: A little sea princess, longing to be human, trades her mermaid's tail for legs,
hoping to win the love of a prince and earn an immortal soul for herself.
[1. Fairy tales. 2. Mermaids—Fiction. I. Andersen, H. C. (Hans Christian), 1805–1875. Lille hafvue. English. II. Title.
PZ8.I763Lt  1998  [E]—dc21  97-9613  CIP  AC  ISBN 0-399-22813-6

This edition ISBN 0-698-11829-4

Printed in the United States of America
Set in Simoncini Garamond

*The art was done in watercolor on Strathmore 500 Bristol.*

Once there was a little mermaid. She lived in the castle of her father, the sea king, with five sisters and their grandmother.

The little mermaid dreamed of the day she would turn fifteen and be old enough to visit the world above the waves. But the little mermaid was the youngest, and had the longest to wait. How she envied her sisters as each in turn became fifteen and traveled to the world above. Each returned with exciting tales to tell.

Finally the day of her fifteenth birthday arrived. She rose to the surface as light as a bubble. In the glow of sunset, a great ship lay anchored.

Curious to see the great ship, she swam right up to a porthole. And there, just inside, she saw a young prince in the midst of celebration, for it was his fifteenth birthday, too. His beauty touched her in a way she had never felt before.

As often happens at sea, suddenly a storm took hold. The ship tossed and pitched in waves that rose like huge mountains. When the doomed ship split in two, the little mermaid could think only of the prince and the fate that might befall him. She dove deep down and frantically searched the turbulent water until she found him. He was not swimming any longer, so she carried him to the surface and cradled his head above the water.

She stayed with him through the night. His eyes never opened. When morning came, the storm had passed, and the two drifted slowly toward land.

When they reached shore, the little mermaid rested the prince's head on the warm sand.

Just then a bell rang and a group of girls came out of a white building nearby. The little mermaid quickly kissed the prince's forehead and found a place to hide. The prince began to revive just as one of the girls came to his side. All the little mermaid could do was watch as the prince smiled at the girl he must have thought had saved him.

With a pain in her heart and a last glance toward the prince, she returned to her home in the sea.

As time passed, the little mermaid could not forget the prince. Her grandmother explained to her that unlike mermaids, who live for three hundred years and then become foam on the sea, humans have souls that live forever in the heavens after death. The little mermaid asked if she too could have such a soul, and her grandmother replied, "Only if you marry a human and he vows to love you forever. But," she explained, "this can never happen, for humans think our pretty tails ugly and prefer their legs."

Although one of her sisters had told her of the magnificent palace in which the prince lived, the little mermaid had no hope of ever being with him. So she made up her mind to ask the dreaded witch of the sea for help. The sea witch lived where the little mermaid had never dared venture before. Her heart pounded with fear as she headed into the sea witch's lair, and she was about to turn back, when suddenly through the mist the monstrous sea witch appeared.

"I know what you want," the sea witch said, cackling horribly, "and I will help you, for it will bring you misfortune! I will give you a potion that will change your tail into a pair of legs. But every time you take a step, it will hurt as though sharp swords are slicing through your feet. And if you do not win your prince's love and he marries someone else, you will turn to sea foam the morning after his wedding. You will not be able to speak, for I will cut out your little tongue as my payment. Do you agree to all of this?" Thinking only of the prince and the immortal soul, the little mermaid agreed.

As the little mermaid swam away, she blew a thousand kisses toward her home, knowing she would never return. She swam to the prince's palace, and drank the potion. The burning liquid seared through her delicate body, and she fainted and lay as though dead.

When the sun rose, the little mermaid slowly opened her eyes. Standing above her was the prince. He asked who she was and how she got there, but alas, she could not speak. She could only look sadly and lovingly at his beautiful face. He took her by the hand and led her into his palace. Every step felt as though she were treading on sharp knives, but she looked at the prince and smiled.

As time passed, the prince became fond of the little mermaid. He told her about how he had almost lost his life in a terrible storm, until a lovely girl found him on a faraway shore and rescued him. But he had not seen her since. The little mermaid knew it was *she* who had saved him, and her heart broke with the silence that bound her.

They spent their days together, and the mermaid thought perhaps he was growing to love her. But then one day the prince asked her to be a bridesmaid at his wedding. His parents had arranged for him to marry a princess from a foreign land. The prince told the little mermaid he did not want to marry anyone but the girl he had seen on the faraway shore.

The next day they set sail. The ship docked at the foreign kingdom, and bells rang out. The princess arrived, and immediately the prince recognized her. This was the girl he had been searching for, the one who had found him after the storm!

At the wedding, the little mermaid did not hear the music or see the ceremony. She was thinking of her death and of everything she had so longed for in this world. She knew this was the last night she would ever see the prince, who never guessed how she loved him.

That night, after the prince and his bride went below deck, the little mermaid stood by the ship's rail. She waited for the first light of dawn, for surely death would follow, as the sea witch had foretold.

Just then, her sisters appeared from the waves. "Our dear sister, you can save yourself! We have been to the witch of the sea. You must thrust this knife into the prince's heart before sunrise. When his blood splashes on your feet, they will change back into a tail once more. Then you can come home." And they disappeared.

The little mermaid went below deck. The knife trembled in her hand as she looked at the prince and princess sleeping peacefully. She knelt down beside the bed and touched the prince's face. Then slowly she rose and left.

She threw the knife into the waves. Where it fell, the water turned red as blood. Then she threw herself into the sea and felt her body begin to dissolve into foam.

The sun rose, and its rays fell warm and gentle on the cold sea foam, but the little mermaid had no sense of death. She felt herself rising, higher and higher. Through the mist she heard voices. "To whom am I coming?" the little mermaid asked.

"We are the children of the air," they said, "and we live among the heavens. We gain immortal souls by doing good for three hundred years. Poor little mermaid! You have tried so hard and are so good. Now you can join us and someday earn a soul."

Then the little mermaid lifted her arms to the sun and rose up with the other children of the air. For one moment she looked back at the sea below and saw the prince and his bride on the deck of the ship.

Then she faced the light and rose up into the clouds floating above.

And for the first time in her life she felt joy.